DISNEY
FAIRIES

Tinker Bell's

FAIRYTASTIC
READING ADVENTURE

Tinker Bell's
FAIRYTASTIC
READING ADVENTURE

LITTLE, BROWN AND COMPANY

New York ·: Boston

Little, Brown and Company

Hachette Book Group
1290 Avenue of the Americas, New York, NY 10104

Visit us at lb-kids.com

Little, Brown and Company is a division of Hachette Book Group, Inc.

The Little, Brown name and logo are trademarks of Hachette Book Group, Inc.

The publisher is not responsible for websites (or their content) that are not owned by the publisher.

First Edition: October 2016

The Trouble with Tink originally published in February 2011 by Disney Publishing Worldwide. *Tinker Bell Takes Charge* originally published in July 2006 by Disney Publishing Worldwide.

Library of Congress Control Number: 2016936597

ISBN 978-0-316-31167-0

10 9 8 7 6 5 4 3 2 1

LSC-C

Printed in the United States of America

Tinker Bell's

FAIRYTASTIC
READING ADVENTURE

The Trouble with Tink

Written by
Kiki Thorpe

Chapter 1

One sunny afternoon in Pixie Hollow, Tinker Bell sat in her workshop, frowning at a copper pot. With one hand, she clutched her tinker's hammer, and with the other, she tugged at her blond bangs, which was Tink's habit when she was thinking hard about something. The pot had been squashed nearly flat on one side. Tink was trying to determine how to make it right again.

All around Tink lay her tinkering tools: baskets full of rivets, scraps of tin, pliers, iron wire, and swatches of steel wool for scouring a pot until it shone. On the walls hung portraits of some of the pans and ladles and washtubs Tink had mended. Tough jobs were always Tink's favorites.

Tink was a pots-and-pans fairy, and her greatest joy came from fixing things. She loved anything metal that could be cracked or dented. Even her workshop was made from a teakettle that had once belonged to a Clumsy.

Ping! Ping! Ping! Tink began to pound away. Beneath Tink's hammer, the copper moved as easily as if she were smoothing the folds in a blanket. Tink had almost finished when a shadow fell across her worktable. She looked up and saw a dark figure silhouetted in the sunny doorway. The edges of the silhouette sparkled.

"Oh, hi, Terence. Come in," said Tink.

Terence moved out of the sunlight and into the room, but he continued to shimmer. Terence was a dust-talent sparrow man. He measured and handed out the fairy dust that allowed Never Land's fairies to fly and do their magic. As a result, he was dustier than most fairies, and he sparkled all the time.

"Hi, Tink. I see you're working. Are you almost done? That's a nice pot," Terence said, all in a rush.

"It's Violet's pot. They're dyeing spider silk tomorrow, and she needs it for boiling the dye," Tink replied.

"That's right, tomorrow is dyeing day," said Terence. "Anyway, Tink, I just wanted to let you know that they're starting a game of tag in the meadow. I thought maybe you'd like to join in."

Tink's wing tips quivered. It had been ages since there had been a game of fairy tag.

She glanced down at the pot again. The dent was nearly smooth. Tink thought she could easily play a game of tag and still have time to finish her work before dinner. Standing up, she slipped her tinker's hammer into a loop on her belt and smiled at Terence. "Let's go," she said.

When Tink and Terence got to the meadow, the game of tag was already in full swing. Fairy tag is different from the sort of tag that humans, or Clumsies, as the fairies call them, play. For one thing, the fairies fly rather than run. For another, the fairies don't just chase each other until one is tagged "it." If that were the case, the fast-flying-talent fairies would win every time.

In fairy tag, the fairies and sparrow men all use their talents to try to win. And when a fairy is tagged, by being tapped on her head and told "Choose you," that fairy's whole talent group becomes "chosen." Games of fairy tag are large, complicated, and very exciting.

As Tink and Terence joined the game, a huge drop of water came hurtling through the air at them. The water-talent fairies were "chosen," Tink realized.

As they sped through the tall grass, the water fairies hurled balls of water at the other fairies. When the balls hit, they burst like water balloons and dampened the fairies' wings. This slowed them down, which helped the water fairies gain on them. Already the other talents had organized their defense. Tink saw that the pots-and-pans fairies had used washtubs to create makeshift catapults. They were trying to catch the balls of water and fling them back at the water fairies.

As Tink zipped down to join them, she heard a voice above her call, "Watch out, Tinker Bell! I'll choose you!" She looked up. Her friend Rani, a water-talent fairy, was circling above her on the back of a dove. Rani was the only fairy in the kingdom who didn't have wings. Brother Dove did her flying for her.

Rani lifted her arm and hurled a water ball. It wobbled through the air and splashed harmlessly on the ground, inches away from Tink. Tink laughed, and so did Rani.

Just then, the pots-and-pans fairies fired a catapult. The water flew at Rani and drenched her. Rani laughed even harder.

"Choose you!" All the fairies stopped midflight and turned. A water-talent fairy named Tally was standing over Jerome, a dust-talent sparrow man. Her hand was on his head.

"Dust talent!" Jerome sang out.

The fairies rearranged themselves. Anyone who happened to be near a dust-talent fairy immediately darted away. Tink caught sight of Terence near a tree stump a few feet away. She bolted. In a flash, Terence was after her. Tink dove into an azalea bush. Terence was right on her heels. She made a hairpin turn around a thick branch. Then she dashed toward an opening in the leaves and headed back to the open meadow. But suddenly, the twigs in front of her closed like a gate. With a flick of fairy dust, Terence had closed the branches of the bush. Tink was trapped. She turned as Terence flew up to her.

Just then, a shout rang out across the meadow: "Hawk!"

At once, Tink and Terence dropped down under the azalea bush's branches. Through the leaves, Tink could see the other fairies ducking for cover. The scout who had spotted the hawk hid in the branches of a nearby elm tree. The entire meadow seemed to hold its breath as the hawk's shadow moved across it.

When it was gone, the fairies waited a few moments, then slowly came out of their hiding places. But the mood had changed. The game of tag was over. Tink and Terence climbed out of the bush.

"I must finish Violet's pot before dinner," Tink told Terence. "Thank you for telling me about the game."

"I'm really glad you came, Tink," said Terence. He gave her a sparkling smile, but Tink didn't see it. She was already flying away, thinking about the copper pot.

As she neared her workshop, she reached for her tinker's hammer hanging on her belt. Her fingertips touched the leather loop, but no hammer. Tink stopped flying. Frantically, she ran her fingers over the belt loop again and again. Her hammer was gone.

Chapter 2

Tink skimmed over the ground, back the way she'd come. Her eyes darted this way and that. She was hoping to catch a glimmer of metal in the tall grass.

When she reached the meadow, her heart sank. To Tink, the meadow looked huge. How would she ever find her hammer in there?

Feeling determined, Tink flew across the open meadow. She tried to recall her zigzagging path in the tag game. Eventually, she gave that up and began to search the meadow inch by inch, flying close to the ground. She looked everywhere she could think of, even places she knew the hammer couldn't possibly be.

As Tink searched, the sun sank into a red pool on the horizon, then disappeared. A thin sliver of moon rose in the sky. The night was so dark that even if Tink had flown over the hammer, she wouldn't have been able to see it. But the hammer was already long gone. A Never crow had spotted it hours before and, attracted by its shine, had carried it off to its nest.

The grass was heavy with dew by the time Tink slowly started back to the Home Tree. *What will I do without my hammer?* Tink wondered. It was her most important tool. She thought of the copper pot waiting for her in her workshop, and tears sprang to her eyes.

It might seem that it should have been easy for Tink to get another tinker's hammer, but in fact, it was not. In the fairy kingdom, there is just the right amount of everything—no more, no less. A tool-making fairy would need Never iron to make a new hammer. And a mining-talent fairy would have to collect the iron. Because their work was difficult, the mining-talent fairies only mined once in a moon cycle, when the moon was full. Tink eyed the thin silver slice in the sky. Judging from the moon, that wouldn't be for many days.

For a pots-and-pans fairy, going many days without fixing pots or pans would be like not eating or sleeping. But that wasn't the only reason Tink was upset. She had a secret. She *did* have a spare hammer. But it was at Peter Pan's hideout—she had accidentally left it there quite a while before. And she was terribly scared about going back to get it.

Tink got back to the Home Tree, but instead of going, she flew up to the highest branch and perched there. She looked up at the stars and tried to figure out what to do.

Tink thought about Peter Pan: his wild red hair, his freckled nose turned up just so, his eyes that looked so happy when he laughed. Tink's heart ached. Remembering Peter Pan was something she almost never let herself do. Since he had brought the Wendy to Never Land, Tink and Peter had hardly spoken.

No, Tink decided. She couldn't go to Peter's for the spare hammer. It would make her too sad. "I'll make do without it," she told herself. What was a hammer, after all, but just another tool?

Chapter 3

The next morning, Tink woke before the other fairies. She crept out of the Home Tree and flew down to the beach. In one corner of the lagoon, there was a small cave that could only be entered at low tide. Tink flew in and landed on the damp ground. The floor of the cave was covered with sea-polished pebbles. Tink carefully picked her way through the rocks. At last Tink picked up a reddish pebble the size and shape of a sunflower seed. *This might work*, Tink thought.

She flew out of the cave, gripping the pebble in her fist. Back in her workshop, Tink used iron wire to bind the flat side of the rock to a twig. With a pinch of fairy dust, she tightened the wires so the rock was snug against the wood. She held up her makeshift hammer and looked at it. "It's not so bad," she said.

Taking a deep breath, Tink began to tap the copper pot.

Clank! Clank! Clank! Tink winced as the horrible sound echoed through her workshop. "I'm sorry, I'm sorry!" Tink whispered to the pot. She tried to tap more gently. The work took forever. Each strike with the pebble hammer left a tiny dent. Slowly, the bent copper straightened out.

But the pot's smooth, shiny surface was now as pitted as the skin of a grapefruit.

It's no good, Tink thought. *This pebble doesn't work at all!* She raised her arm to give the pot one last tap. Just then, the pebble flew off the stick and landed with a clatter in a pile of tin scrap, as if to say it agreed.

Suddenly, the door of Tink's workshop burst open and a fairy flew in. She wore a gauzy dress tie-dyed in a fancy pattern of blues and greens. Her cheeks were bright splotches of pink. Corkscrews of curly red hair stood out in all directions from her head, and her hands were stained purple with berry juice. It was Violet, the pot's owner, a dyeing-talent fairy.

"Tink! Are you done with my pot yet?" Violet asked.

"Oh, Violet, hi. Yes, I'm, er...I'm almost done with the pot..." Tink said.

"It looks...uh..." Violet's voice trailed off as she eyed the battered pot. Tink was the best pots-and-pans fairy in the kingdom. Violet didn't want to sound as if she were criticizing her work.

"It needs a couple of touch-ups, but I fixed the squashed part," Tink said. "It's perfectly good for boiling dye in. We can try it now if you like."

The door of Tink's workshop opened again. Terence came in, carrying a ladle that was so twisted it looked as if it had been tied in a knot. "Hi, Tink! I brought you a ladle to fix!" he called out. "Oh, hello, Violet! Dropping off?" he asked as he spied the copper pot.

"No...er, picking up," Violet said worriedly.

"Oh," said Terence. He looked back at the pot in surprise.

Tink filled a bucket with water from a rain barrel outside her workshop and brought it over to her worktable. As Violet and Terence watched, she poured the water into the copper pot.

"See?" Tink said to Violet. "It's good as—"

Just then, they heard a metallic creaking sound. *Plink, plink, plink, plink!* One by one, tiny streams of water burst through the damaged copper.

"Oh!" Violet and Terence gasped. They turned to Tink, their eyes wide.

Tink felt herself blush, but she couldn't

tear her eyes away from the leaking pot. She had never failed to fix a pot before, much less made it worse than it was when she got it.

The thing was, no fairy ever failed at her talent. To do so would mean you weren't really talented at all.

Chapter 4

Violet left quickly after that, saying she would share a dye pot with another fairy and would come back later for her pot.

Terence, meanwhile, could see that Tink was upset and did his best to cheer her up.

"Maybe you need to take a break," he suggested. "Why don't we fly to the tearoom? On my way here, I smelled pumpkin muffins baking in the kitchen. They smelled deli—"

"I'm not hungry," Tink interrupted, although she was starving. She hadn't had breakfast, or dinner the night before. But the talents always sat together in the tea-room. Tink didn't feel like sitting at a table with the other pots-and-pans fairies right now.

"Is everything all right?" Terence asked, setting the twisted ladle down on Tink's workbench.

"I can't talk today, Terence," Tink snapped. She knew she wasn't being fair. But she was upset and embarrassed. "I have a lot of work, and I'm already behind."

"Oh." Terence's shoulders sagged. "Just let me know if you need anything."

As soon as Terence was gone, Tink flew to a nearby birch tree where a carpenter-talent sparrow man worked and asked if she could borrow his hammer. The sparrow man agreed, provided that she brought it back in two days' time. Tink promised she would.

Two days. Tink didn't know what she'd do after that. But she wasn't going to think about it, she decided. Not just yet.

When Tink entered her empty workshop, she spied a plate with a pumpkin muffin on it and a cup of buttermilk on her workbench.

Terence, Tink thought. She was sorry that she'd snapped at him earlier.

As soon as she'd eaten, Tink felt better. She picked up the carpenter's hammer and began to work on a stack of pie pans. Dulcie, the baking-talent fairy who'd brought them to her, complained that the pies she baked in them kept burning. Tink thought it had something to do with the pans' shape, or maybe the tin on the bottom of the pans was too thin.

The carpenter's hammer was almost twice as big as her tinker's hammer. Holding it in her hand, Tink felt as clumsy as a Clumsy. Still, it was much better than the pebble.

Tink worked slowly with the awkward hammer. She reshaped the pie pans, then added an extra layer of tin to the bottom of each one. When she was done, she looked over her work. *It's not the best job I've ever done*, she thought. *But it's not so bad, either.*

Tink gathered the pie pans into a stack and carried them to Dulcie, who was delighted to have them back. "Don't miss tea this afternoon, Tink," she said with a wink as she brushed flour from her hands.

"We're making strawberry pie. I'll save you an extra-big slice!"

On the way back to her workshop, Tink ran into Prilla, an excitable young fairy.

"Tink!" Prilla cried. "Did you hear?"

"Hear what?" asked Tink.

"About Queen Clarion's tub! It's sprung a leak!"

Tink's eyes widened. The bathtub was one of Queen Clarion's most prized possessions. It was the size of a coconut shell and made of Never pewter, with morning glory leaves sculpted into its sides. The tub rested on four feet shaped like lions' paws, and there were two notches at the back where the queen could rest her wings to keep them dry while she took her bath. Tink would love to work on the bathtub.

"The queen's attendants looked all over,

but they couldn't spot the leak. I thought of you when I heard, Tink," Prilla said. "Of course, the queen will want you to fix it. You're the best." Prilla grinned at Tink.

Tink grinned back. It was the first time she'd smiled since she lost her hammer. "I hope so, Prilla. It would be quite an honor to work on the queen's tub," she replied.

"See you later, Tink!" Prilla called as she flew off.

Tink thought about the queen's tub all afternoon as she fixed the spout on a tea-kettle that wouldn't whistle. What kind of leak could it be? By the time Tink had finished fixing the kettle, it was nearly tea-time. "They'll need this in the kitchen," Tink said to herself as she buffed the tea-kettle with a piece of suede. She would take it to the kitchen, then go to the tearoom for strawberry pie. Tink's stomach rumbled hungrily at the thought. But when she got to the kitchen, a horrible smell greeted her. Tink quickly handed the teakettle to one of the cooking-talent fairies and held both hands to her nose.

"What is that smell?" she asked the fairy.

But the fairy just gave her a strange look and hurried off to fill the teakettle with water.

Tink made her way through the kitchen until she found Dulcie. She was standing over several steaming pies that had just been pulled from the oven. She looked as if she might cry.

"Dulcie, what's going on?" Tink asked.

As soon as Dulcie saw Tink, her forehead wrinkled. "Oh, Tink. I don't know how to tell you this, but it's the pies. They're all coming out mincemeat."

Tink turned and looked at the steaming pies. That was where the horrible smell was coming from.

"We tried everything," Dulcie went on. "When the strawberry came out all wrong, we tried plum. When that didn't work, we tried cherry. But every time we pulled the pies out of the oven, they'd turned into mincemeat."

This was indeed a kitchen disaster. Fairies hate mincemeat. To them it tastes like burned broccoli and old socks.

"Is there something wrong with the oven?" Tink asked Dulcie.

"No, Tink," Dulcie said. "It's the pans you fixed. Only the pies baked in those pans are the ones that get spoiled."

Chapter 5

ink's mind reeled. But before she could say anything, a shrill whistle split the air. The tea water had boiled. A cooking-talent sparrow man hurried over to lift the kettle off the fire. Expertly, the sparrow man poured the water into the teacups until there wasn't a drop left. But the teakettle continued to shriek. The sparrow man lifted the kettle's lid and a puff of steam escaped, but the kettle still whistled on. Without pausing, it changed pitch and began to whistle an earsplitting melody.

All the fairies in the kitchen, including Tink, covered their ears. Several fairies from other talents who were in the tearoom poked their heads in the door of the kitchen.

"What's all that noise?" a garden-talent fairy asked one of the baking-talent fairies.

"It's the teakettle, the one that just wouldn't whistle," the baking-talent fairy replied. "Tink fixed it, and now it won't shut up!"

"And the pie pans Tink fixed aren't any good, either," another baking-talent fairy noted over the noise. "Every pie baked in them turns into mincemeat!"

A murmur went around the room. Everyone turned and looked at Tink.

Tink stared back at them, blushing so deeply her glow turned orange. Then, without thinking, she turned and fled.

✦   ✦   ✦

Tink was sitting in the shade of a wild rosebush, deep in thought. She didn't notice Vidia, a fast-flying-talent fairy, flying overhead. Suddenly, Vidia landed right in front of Tink.

"Tinker Bell, darling," Vidia greeted her.

"Hello, Vidia," Tink replied. Of all the fairies in the kingdom, Vidia was the one Tink liked the least. Vidia was selfish and mean-spirited, and at the moment she was smiling in a way Tink didn't like at all.

"I'm so *sorry* to hear about your trouble," Vidia said.

"It's nothing," Tink said. "I was just flustered. I'll go back to the kitchen and fix the teakettle now."

"Oh, don't worry about that. Angus was in the tearoom," Vidia said. Angus was a pots-and-pans sparrow man. "He got the teakettle to shut up. No, Tink, what I meant was, I'm sorry to hear about your *talent*."

Tink blinked. "What do you mean?"

"Oh, don't you know?" Vidia asked. "Everyone's talking about it. The rumor flying around the kingdom is that you've lost your talent."

"What?" Tink leaped to her feet.

"Oh, it's such a *shame*," Vidia added, shaking her head.

"I haven't lost my talent," Tink growled.

"Well, you have to admit, your work

hasn't exactly been...*inspired* lately. Why, even I could fix pots and pans better than that," Vidia said with a little laugh. "But I wouldn't worry too much. I'm sure they won't make you leave the fairy kingdom *forever*, even if your talent has dried up for good."

Tink looked at her coldly. "I'm sure that would never happen, Vidia."

"But no one really knows, do they?" Vidia replied with a pitying smile. "After all, no fairy has ever lost her talent before. But I guess we'll soon find out. You see, I've come with a message. The queen would like to see you."

Tink's stomach did a little flip. The queen?

"She's in the gazebo," Vidia told her. "I'll let you fly there on your own. I expect you'll want to collect your thoughts. Good-bye, Tink." And then finally, Vidia flew away.

Tink's heart raced. Was it really possible that she could be banished from the kingdom for losing her talent?

But I haven't lost my talent! Tink thought indignantly. *I've just lost my hammer.*

With that thought in mind, Tink took a deep breath, lifted her chin, and flew off to meet the queen.

Chapter 6

The queen's gazebo sat high on a rock overlooking the fairy kingdom. Tink landed lightly on a bed of soft moss outside the entrance. All around her she heard the jingle of seashell wind chimes, which hung around the gazebo. Inside, the gazebo was drenched in purple from the sunlight filtering through the violet petals that made up the roof. Soft, fresh fir needles carpeted the floor and gave off a piney scent.

Queen Clarion stood at one of the open windows. She was looking out at the glittering blue water of the Mermaid Lagoon, which lay in the distance beyond the fairy kingdom. When she heard Tink, she turned.

"Tinker Bell, come in," said the queen. "How are you feeling?"

"I'm fine," Tink replied.

"Are you sleeping well?" asked the queen.

"Well enough," Tink told her.

"No cough? Your glow hasn't changed color?" asked the queen.

"No," Tink replied. Suddenly, she realized that the queen was checking her for signs of fairy distemper. It was a rare illness but very contagious. If Tink had it, she would have to be separated from the group

to keep from making the whole fairy kingdom sick.

"No, I'm fine," Tink repeated to reassure
her. "I feel very well. Really."

When the queen heard this, she seemed
to relax. It was just the slightest change in
her posture, but Tink noticed, and she, too,
breathed a sigh of relief. *The queen won't
banish me*, Tink thought.

"Tink, you know there are rumors..."
Queen Clarion hesitated. She was reluctant
to repeat them.

"They say I've lost my talent," Tink said
quickly so that the queen wouldn't have to.
"It's nasty gossip—and untrue. It's just that—"
Tink stopped. She tugged at her bangs.

She was afraid that if she told Queen
Clarion about her missing hammer, the
queen would think she was irresponsible.

The queen waited for Tink to go on. When she didn't, the queen walked closer to her and looked into her blue eyes. "Tink," she said, "is there anything you want to tell me?"

She asked so gently that Tink felt the urge to tell her everything—about the pebble hammer and the carpenter's hammer and even about Peter Pan. But Tink had never told another fairy about Peter, and she was afraid to now.

Besides, Tink told herself, *the queen has more important things to worry about than a missing hammer.*

Tink shook her head. "No," she said. "I'm sorry my pots and pans haven't been very good lately. I'll try to do better."

The queen looked carefully at her. She knew something was wrong, but she didn't know what. She only knew that Tink didn't want to tell her. "Very well," she said. As Tink turned to leave, she added, "Be good to yourself, Tink."

Outside, Tink felt better. The meeting with the queen had been nothing to worry about. Maybe things weren't as bad as they seemed. *All I have to do now is find a new hammer, and everything will be back to normal*, Tink thought with a burst of confidence.

"Tink!" someone called.

She looked down and saw Rani and Prilla standing near a puddle. Tink flew down and joined them. As she landed, she saw that Rani was crying.

"I'm so sorry, Tink," Rani said. She pulled a damp leafkerchief from one of her many pockets and blew her nose into it. As a water fairy, Rani cried a lot and was always prepared. "About your talent, I mean."

Tink's smile faded. "There's nothing to be sorry about. There's nothing wrong with my talent," she said irritably.

"Don't worry, Tink," Prilla said. "I know how you feel. When I thought I didn't have a talent, it was awful." Prilla hadn't known what her talent was when she first arrived in Never Land. She'd had to figure it out on her own. "Maybe you just need to try lots of things," she advised Tink, "and then it will come to you."

"I already have a talent, Prilla," Tink said carefully.

"But maybe you need another talent, like a backup when the one you have isn't working," Prilla went on. "What do you think, Rani?"

But Rani just sniffled helplessly.

"Anyway, Tink," said Prilla, "I wouldn't worry too much about what everyone is saying about—"

"Dinner?" Rani cut Prilla off.

Prilla looked at her. "No, I meant—"

"Yes, about dinner," Rani interrupted again, more firmly. She had dried her eyes and now she was looking hard at Prilla. Rani could see that the topic of talents was upsetting Tink, and she wanted Prilla to be quiet. "It's time, isn't it?"

"Yes," said Tink. But she wasn't looking at Rani and Prilla. Her mind seemed to be somewhere else altogether.

Rani put her fingers to her mouth and

whistled. They heard the sound of wings beating overhead. A moment later, Brother Dove landed on the ground next to Rani. He would take her to the tearoom. But before Rani had even climbed onto his back, Tink took off in the direction of the Home Tree without another word. Rani and Prilla had no choice but to follow.

Chapter 7

When they reached the tearoom, Tink said good-bye to Rani and Prilla. Rani was going to sit with the other water-talent fairies, and Prilla was joining her. Since Prilla didn't have her own talent group, she was an honorary member of many different talents, and she sat at a different table every night. Tonight she would sit with the water-talent fairies and practice making fountains in her soup.

Tink made her way over to a table under a large chandelier where the pots-and-pans fairies sat together for their meals. As she took her seat, the other fairies at the table barely looked up.

"It's a crack in the bottom, I'll bet," a fairy named Zuzu was saying.

"But don't you think it could be something around the drain, since the water leaked out so quickly?" asked Angus, the sparrow man who had fixed the whistling teakettle in the kitchen earlier that day.

A serving-talent fairy with a large soup tureen walked over to the table and began to ladle chestnut dumpling soup into the fairies' bowls. Tink noticed with pride that the ladle was one she had once repaired. She leaned forward. "What's everyone talking about?" she asked. The other fairies turned, as if noticing for the first time that Tink was sitting there.

"About the queen's bathtub," Zuzu explained. "She's asked us to come fix it tomorrow. We're trying to guess what's wrong with it."

"Oh, yes!" said Tink. "I've been thinking about that, too. It might be a pinprick hole. Those are the sneakiest sorts of leaks—the water just sort of drizzles out one drop at a time." Tink laughed, but no one joined her. She looked around the table. The other fairies were staring at her or looking awkwardly down at their soup bowls. Suddenly, Tink realized that the queen had said nothing to her about the bathtub that afternoon in the gazebo.

"Tink," another fairy named Copper said gently, "we've all agreed that Angus and Zuzu should be the ones to repair the tub, since they are the most talented pots-and-pans fairies... lately, that is."

"Oh!" said Tink. "Of course." She swallowed hard.

Now all the pots-and-pans fairies were looking at Tink with a mixture of love and concern. And, Tink was sad to see, pity. *I could just tell everyone that I lost my hammer*, Tink thought. *But if they asked about the spare...*

Tink couldn't finish the thought. She knew her time with Peter Pan was something the other pots-and-pans fairies would never understand.

At last the fairies changed the topic and began to talk about the leaky pots and broken teakettles they'd fixed that day. As they chattered and laughed, Tink silently ate her soup. As soon as she was done, Tink put down her spoon and slipped away from the table. The other pots-and-pans fairies were so busy talking, they didn't notice her leaving.

Outside, Tink returned to the topmost branches of the Home Tree, where she'd sat the night before. She didn't want to go back to her workshop—there were pots and pans still waiting to be fixed. She didn't want to go to her room, either. It seemed too lonely there. At least here she had the stars to keep her company.

"Maybe it's true that I've lost my talent," Tink said to the stars. "If I don't have a hammer, then I can't fix things. And if I can't fix things, it's just like having no talent at all." The stars only twinkled in reply.

From where she was sitting, Tink could

see the hawthorn tree where Mother Dove lived. Between its branches, she could make out the faint shape of Mother Dove's nest. Mother Dove was the only creature in the fairy kingdom who knew all about Tink and Peter Pan. What a comfort it would be to go to Mother Dove. She would know what to do. But something held Tink back. She remembered Mother Dove's words to her on her very first day in Never Land: *You're Tinker Bell, sound and fine as a bell. Shiny and jaunty as a new pot. Brave enough for anything, the most courageous fairy to come in a long year.* Tink had felt so proud that day.

But Tink didn't feel very brave right now, certainly not brave enough to go to Peter's and get her spare hammer. He was only a boy, but still she couldn't find the courage.

Tink couldn't bear the idea that Mother Dove would think she wasn't brave or sound or fine. It would be worse than losing her talent.

"Tink," said a voice.

Tink turned. Terence was standing behind her on the branch.

"I haven't fixed the ladle yet," Tink told him miserably.

"I didn't come because of the ladle," Terence replied. "I saw you leave the tearoom."

Terence sat down next to her on the branch. "Tink, are you all right? Everyone is saying that..." He paused. Like Queen Clarion, Terence couldn't bring himself to repeat the gossip. It seemed too unkind.

"That I've lost my talent," Tink finished for him. She sighed. "Maybe they're right, Terence. I can't seem to fix anything.

Everything I touch comes out worse than when I started."

Terence was startled. One thing he had always admired about Tink was her fierceness. He had never seen her look as defeated as she did now.

"I don't believe that," he told her. "You're the best pots-and-pans fairy in the kingdom. Talent doesn't just go away like that."

Tink said nothing. But she felt grateful to him for still believing in her.

"Tink," Terence asked gently, "what's really going on?"

Tink hesitated. "I lost my hammer," she blurted at last.

As soon as the words left her lips, Tink felt relieved. It was as if she'd let out a huge breath that she'd been holding in.

"Is that all it is?" Terence said. He almost laughed. "You could just borrow a hammer," he suggested.

Tink told Terence about the hammer she'd made from a pebble and the one she'd borrowed from the carpenter fairy. "Neither of them works," she explained. "I need a tinker's hammer."

"Maybe there's a spare—" Terence began.

"I *have* a spare," Tink wailed. "But I left it at Peter Pan's hideout."

"He won't give it back?" asked Terence.

Tink shook her head. "I haven't asked." She looked away.

Terence didn't know much about Peter Pan, only that Tink had been friends with him and then—suddenly—she wasn't. But he saw that Tink was upset and ashamed, and he didn't ask her anything more.

"I could go with you," Terence said at last. "To Peter Pan's, I mean."

Tink's mind raced. Perhaps if someone else came along, it wouldn't be so hard to see Peter... "You would do that?" she asked.

"Tink," said Terence, "I'm your friend. You don't even need to ask."

He gave Tink a sparkling smile. This time, Tink saw it and she smiled back.

Chapter 8

*E*arly the next morning, before most of the fairy kingdom was awake, Tink rapped at the door of Terence's room. She wanted to leave for Peter's hideout before she lost her nerve altogether.

Terence threw open the door after the first knock. He grinned at Tink. "Ready to go get your talent back, Tinker Bell?"

Tink smiled. She was glad Terence was going with her. They left Pixie Hollow just as the sun's rays shone over Torth Mountain.

"See that stream?" Tink asked, pointing to a silver ribbon of water winding through the forest below. "It leads to an underground cavern that's filled with gold and silver. Captain Hook and his men have hidden away a whole pirate ship's worth of treasure there."

"You must know Never Land better than any fairy in the kingdom," Terence said admiringly.

Tink looked at the island below her and felt a little twinge of pride. What Terence said was true. With Peter, Tink had explored nearly every inch of Never Land. Every rock, meadow, and hill reminded her of some adventure. Of course, they also reminded her of Peter.

Tink felt a flutter of nervousness. How

would it be to see him? What if the Wendy was there, or Peter had found someone else to play with? What if he ignored her again?

When Tink reached the densest, darkest part of the forest, she began to glide down in a spiral. Terence followed her.

They plunged through a canopy of fig trees and landed on a white-speckled mushroom. The mushroom was nearly as wide as a Clumsy's dinner plate. "It's Peter's hideout," Tink explained. "They use a mushroom cap to disguise the chimney to fool Captain Hook."

After they'd rested for a moment, Tink sprang from the mushroom and flew up to a hollow in the trunk of a nearby jackfruit tree. She was about to dive inside when Terence grabbed her wrist.

"What about owls?" he said worriedly.

If there was an owl living in the hollow, it might eat them.

Tink laughed. "Anything that lived here would be terrorized by the Lost Boys. This is the entrance to the hideout!"

Peeking inside, Terence saw the entire tree was hollow, right to its roots. He followed Tink as she flew down the trunk. They came out in an underground room.

Terence looked around. The floor and walls were made of packed earth. Tree roots hung down from the ceiling, and from these, string hammocks dangled limply. Here and there on the ground lay slingshots, socks, and dirty coconut-shell bowls. The remains of a fire smoldered in a corner. The hideout was empty.

He's not home, Tink thought. She felt both disappointed and relieved.

Just then, they heard whistling coming from somewhere near the back of the den.

Tink and Terence flew toward the sound. Their glows made two bright spots of light in the dim room.

At the back of the hideout, they spied a nook that was tucked out of sight from the rest of the room. The whistling was coming from there.

When they rounded the corner, Terence saw a freckled boy with a mop of red hair sitting on a stool formed by a thick, twisted root. In one hand he held a jackknife, and he whistled as he worked it over a piece of wood. A fishing pole leaned against the wall behind him. Looking more closely, Terence saw that the boy was carving a fishing hook big enough to catch a whale.

Tink saw her old friend, Peter Pan.

Taking a deep breath, she said, "Hello, Peter."

But Peter didn't seem to hear her. He continued to whistle and chip at the wood. Tink flew a little bit closer. "Peter!" she exclaimed.

Peter kept on whistling and whittling. Was he be angry with her? Tink wondered with a sudden shock. The thought had never occurred to her. She hovered, unsure what to do.

Then Terence took her hand. They flew up to Peter until they were just a few inches from his face. "Peter!" they both cried.

Peter lifted his head. When he saw them, a bright smile lit his face. Tink smiled, too.

"Hello! What's this?" Peter said. "Two butterflies have come to visit me! Are you lost, butterflies?"

Tink's smile faded. She and Terence stared at Peter. *Butterflies?* Tink thought, *Has he forgotten me already?*

Peter squinted at them. "I just love butterflies," he said. "You'd make a fine addition to my collection. Let's see now, where are my pins?" He began to search his pockets.

"Here it is!" he cried. He held up a straight pin with a colored bulb on the end. It was big enough to skewer a butterfly—or a fairy—right through the middle.

"Now hold still," Peter said. Gripping the pin in one hand, he reached up to grab Tink and Terence with the other.

"Fly!" Terence screamed to Tink.

Just before Peter's stubby fingers closed around them, the fairies turned and fled toward the exit.

Chapter 9

But as they reached the roots of the jackfruit tree, they heard a whoop of laughter behind them. Tink stopped and glanced back over her shoulder. Peter was shaking with laughter.

"Oh, Tink!" he gasped. "You should have seen the looks on your faces. Butterflies! Oh, I am funny!" He bent over as another round of laughter seized him. Terence, who had been just ahead of Tink, also stopped and turned. Frowning, he came to hover next to her. He had never met Peter Pan face-to-face before, and he was starting to think that he wasn't going to like him very much. But Tink was smiling. It had only been a joke! Peter *did* remember her!

At last Peter stopped laughing. He bounded up to Tink and Terence, his eyes shining.

"Tink!" he cried. "It's awful great to see you. Where've you been hiding?"

"Hello, Peter," Tink replied. "Meet my friend Terence."

"A boy pixie! Fantastic!" Peter cried. The grin on his face was so wide and enthusiastic that Terence's heart softened. The thing was, it was impossible not to like Peter Pan. He had the eagerness of a puppy, the cleverness of a fox, and the freedom of a lark— all rolled into one spry, redheaded boy.

"You'll never guess what I've got, Tink. Come see!" He said it as if Tink had been away for a mere few hours and had now come back to play.

Peter led Tink and Terence over to a corner of the hideout and pulled a wooden box out of a hole in the wall. "I keep my most important things in my treasure chest," Peter explained to Terence, gesturing to the box. He lifted the lid of the cigar box. "Now . . ." Reaching inside, he took out a small object. He held it out toward Tink and Terence in the palm of his hand. It was yellowish white and shaped like a triangle, with razor-sharp edges that narrowed to a point.

Tink clasped her hands together. "Oh!" she gasped. "You got it!"

"What is it?" Terence asked.

"A shark's tooth," Peter replied, just a bit smugly. "Isn't it swell? I'm going to put it on a string and make a necklace."

"The first time I met Peter, he was trying to steal a shark's tooth," Tink explained to Terence.

"That's right!" exclaimed Peter. "I'd made a bet with the boys that I could steal a tooth from a live shark. I built a small raft out of birchwood and was paddling out to sea..."

From the way he began, Terence could tell that Peter had told this story many times before, and that he loved telling it. "I had just paddled beyond the reef," Peter continued, "when I felt something bump the underside of my raft."

"The shark?" asked Terence.

Peter nodded. "He was looking for his lunch. But he didn't know that I was looking for him, too!"

"How did you plan to get his tooth?" Terence asked.

"I meant to stun him with my oar, then steal the tooth while he was out cold," said Peter. "But he was bigger than I'd thought, and before I knew it, he'd bitten my little raft right in half! I was sinking fast, and it looked like the end for me, when suddenly I heard a jingling sound over my head. I looked up and there was Tinker Bell. She yelled down at me..."

"'Fly, silly boy!'" Tink and Peter cried together. They laughed, remembering.

"But I didn't know how to fly," Peter told Terence. "So Tink taught me how, right then and there. She sprinkled some fairy dust on me, and before I knew it, I'd zipped up into the air, out of the shark's reach. Boy, was he mad!"

"So, you went back and got the shark tooth this time?" Tink asked Peter, pointing to the tooth in his hand.

Peter shrugged. "Naw. A mermaid gave this to me. But now I'm going to go out and get the whole shark!" He pointed to the fishing pole and the wooden hook he'd been carving.

Tink and Peter both burst out laughing. Just then, Tink caught sight of something in the cigar box. Her eyes widened. "My hammer!" she exclaimed.

"I saved it for you, Tink," Peter said. "I knew you'd be back for it."

Tink reached into the box and picked up the hammer. It fit perfectly in her hand. She tapped it lightly into the palm of her other hand, then closed her eyes and sighed. She felt as if she'd come home after a long, long trip.

Then Tink turned to Peter and said, "It's been so good to see you, Peter. But we have to go back to the fairy kingdom now."

Peter looked at her in surprise. "What? Now? But what about hide-and-seek?"

Tink shook her head. She was glad to realize that she didn't *want* to stay, not for hide-and-seek or anything else. She wanted to get back to Pixie Hollow, back to her pots and pans. That was where she belonged.

Tink flew so close to Peter's face that he

had to cross his eyes to see her. She kissed the bridge of his freckled nose. "I'll come back soon to visit," she promised. And she meant it. Then, taking Terence's hand, she flew back out of the jackfruit tree and into the forest.

Chapter 10

As Tink headed back to the fairy kingdom with Terence, one last thing was bothering her. She didn't want all of Pixie Hollow to know about the hammer and her trip to see Peter. Enough hurtful gossip had already spread through the kingdom. Tink didn't want any more. She wanted to ask Terence if he would keep their trip to Peter's a secret between them. But before she could, he turned to her.

"I don't think anyone else needs to know about this trip, do you?" he asked. "You've got your hammer back, and that's what matters."

Tink grinned and nodded. What a good friend Terence was.

"The only thing is," Terence said, "how will we convince everyone that you have your talent back?"

Tink thought for a moment. "I have an idea," she said.

Putting on a burst of speed, Tink raced Terence all the way back to Pixie Hollow. When they got to the Home Tree, Tink went straight to Queen Clarion's quarters.

"I've come to fix the queen's bathtub," Tink told the attendant who answered the door.

Terence grinned. Tink was clever. This was the perfect way to prove that her talent was back. Terence didn't doubt that Tink could fix the tub. She was the best pots-and-pans fairy in the kingdom. But the attendant hesitated. Everyone had heard about Tink and her talent. She wanted to refuse to let Tink fix it. Just then, the queen stepped forward. She had heard Tink's request. "Come in, Tink," she said.

"I've come to fix your bathtub," Tink repeated to the queen.

Queen Clarion looked at Tink. In Tink's blue eyes, she saw a fierce certainty that hadn't been there the day before, when they'd talked in the gazebo. She nodded. "Take Tink to the bathtub," she told her attendant.

Just before Tink left, Terence grabbed her hand. "Good luck," he said.

Tink held up her hammer and gave his hand a squeeze. "I don't need it!" she said.

Tinker Bell Takes Charge

Written by
Eleanor Fremont

Chapter 1

It was a mild, sunny day in Pixie Hollow—a perfect sort of a day. But even though it was a perfect day, Tinker Bell was not in her usual high spirits. Something was bothering her, but she could not figure out what it was. Just that morning, she had caught sight of her face in the polished walls of the Home Tree's lobby. She'd noticed her slumped shoulders and the frown on her face. Even her ponytail drooped.

This troublesome feeling was on her mind now as she flew toward her bedroom, which was high in the branches of the Home Tree. Tink was heading back there to change her shoes, which had gotten wet during a visit to Thistle's strawberry patch. She headed up through the trunk of the Home Tree and turned right, then left, then left again, winding upward. The corridor narrowed as the tree's limbs tapered.

Tink's bedroom was at the end of one of the topmost branches. As soon as she was inside, her spirits lifted a bit. Tink loved her room. Everything in it reflected her talent and personality. There was her beloved bed, which was made from a pirate's metal loaf pan. There were the lampshades made from old colanders. Even the chair was special. The back of it was made from a serving platter, the seat was a frying pan, and the legs were made from old serving spoons.

At one point or another, Tink had repaired the frying pan, the platter, and each of the spoons. But eventually, pans and spoons wore out, and when that happened, the kitchen fairies threw them away.

Tink felt a special connection with every pot and pan she'd ever fixed. She couldn't bear to see any of them on the scrap-metal heap. So when the pan, the platter, and the spoons were thrown away, Tink had rescued them and brought them back to her workshop. With a lot of thought and a few pinches of fairy dust, she'd turned them into a chair.

Tink thought about the frying-pan chair as she hurriedly pulled on a pair of dry shoes, then closed the door to her room and flew back down through the Home Tree. What a wonderful challenge it had been to make that chair.

Suddenly, Tink stopped in her tracks.

"That's it!" she said aloud. "That is what's bothering me! No challenge!"

Tink was one of the best pots-and-pans-talent fairies in all of Pixie Hollow. Her joy came from fixing things. She liked a challenging problem more than almost anything.

But for weeks now, every job Tink had been given had been as easy as gooseberry pie. No pots that wouldn't boil water. No colanders that refused to drain. No pans that were more hole than pan. Just "fix this little hole, fix that little hole." Boring, boring, boring. *But at least now I know what's wrong*, Tink thought. *What I need is a problem to solve! A big one!*

"Tink!" A voice behind her interrupted her thoughts. Tink turned. Her good friend Rani, a water-talent fairy, was hurrying toward her.

Being the only fairy without wings, Rani could not fly. So Tink gently landed on the moss carpet in the Home Tree's hallway. She waited until Rani caught up.

"Where are you going?" Rani asked.

"I was just on my way back to my workshop," Tink replied. "Why do you—"

"Ask?" said Rani. She had a habit of finishing everyone's sentences. "No big reason. I just thought maybe we could play a game of—"

But Rani never got to finish. At that moment, she was interrupted by a tremendous crash. Both fairies heard branches cracking and snapping near the top of the Home Tree. In the next instant, there was a *thud* that shook the tree to its very roots. Tink and Rani nearly lost their balance. From the nearby tearoom came the sound of dishes falling and shattering.

Then there was silence. Tink and Rani stared at each other. "Did the moon just fall out of the sky?" Rani whispered in awe.

"Maybe it was a branch falling from another tree," said Tink. But even as she spoke, she knew that wasn't it. The sound had been made by something very heavy and solid. And it had landed quite close by.

"Maybe a great big bird just came in for a landing," said Rani.

"Maybe," said Tink. But that didn't seem right either.

The two fairies listened carefully. After a long moment, Tink took a deep breath and straightened her shoulders. "We've got to go and see—"

"What it is. If you say so," said Rani. She dabbed her forehead with a leafkerchief and attempted to smile bravely.

The two fairies headed back toward the front entrance of the Home Tree. Tink walked so that she wouldn't get too far ahead of Rani. Brave as she was, even Tink didn't want to go outside alone. Together they hurried past the tearoom, down the corridor, through the lobby, and out the knothole door.

When Tink stepped into the sunlight, she stopped cold and gasped. Rani, who was right on Tink's heels, crashed into her.

Rani peeked over Tink's shoulder and gasped, too.

"*What* is *that?*" she whispered.

Chapter 2

Right in front of them was a huge, menacing-looking black ball. It was taller than two fairies put together and just as wide. It had landed right in the middle of the Home Tree's courtyard.

A large crack ran through the courtyard where it had smashed down. Several toadstool chairs had been damaged. The ground around the ball was covered with the splintered remains of branches and twigs. Tink's mind reeled. The courtyard was a very special place for the fairies. Many of their most important meetings and celebrations were held there. Not to mention, the fairies had to fly through it to reach the Home Tree's knothole door. Whenever Tink saw the courtyard, she felt that she was home. Now the sight of the damaged courtyard made her heart ache. A large crowd of fairies had gathered around the ball. Clarion, the fairy queen, stepped forward.

"Is everyone all right?" she asked.

Noses and wings were quickly counted, amid a buzz of concern. Incredibly, every fairy in the Home Tree had escaped harm.

The queen sighed with relief. She looked around the crowd. "Terence, Spring, Jerome, Rosetta, Luna," she said. The fairies and sparrow men sprang to attention. "Fly to the top of the tree and see what damage has been done. Please report back at once."

The group took off. When they had gone, a scullery-talent fairy tiptoed up to the great ball. She raised her hand as if to touch its rough surface. But at the last second she pulled her hand back. "Do you think it might be alive?" she whispered.

All at once, the fairies nearest to the ball hopped back a couple of steps.

"What's it made of?" asked Dulcie, a baking-talent fairy.

The fairies around her shook their heads, muttering, "Don't know."

"Maybe it's a big rock," said Angus, a pots-and-pans-talent sparrow man. "Though I've certainly never seen a rock this round before."

"Maybe it's a giant black pearl," said Rani. "Though I've never seen a pearl this big."

Tink shook her head. "No," she said. "It would be shiny if it were a pearl."

Dulcie flew hesitantly up to it. She gave it a small rap with her knuckles. "Ow!" she said. "It's hard!" She blew on her hand. "And it's hot!" she added.

Tink didn't like to stand around. She marched up to the ball and gave it a good hard smack.

"It's iron," she said. She shook her hand to cool it off from the hot metal. "Good old-fashioned Never iron."

Several fairies frowned. "Iron is really heavy," Dulcie said worriedly.

"It's going to be hard to move," said Rani.

"We should try to find out where it came from," the queen told them. "That might help us figure out how to get rid of it."

Her suggestion was greeted with enthusiasm. "Let's take a good look at it," said Rani.

The fairies all moved in closer. "Hold on!" said Tink. She hovered like a hummingbird near the very top of the ball. "I see something."

Other fairies flew over to join her. "You're right," said Lily, a garden-talent fairy. "It's some kind of a mark."

Angus nodded. "It's almost like a—"

"A hook!" Tink shouted in triumph. "It's a mark that looks like a hook! And you know what that means."

"*Captain Hook!*" cried several fairies.

"Of course. Why didn't I realize it before? It's a cannonball!" Tink declared.

Tink had seen plenty of cannonballs back in the days when she had spent time with Peter Pan. But she had never before seen a cannonball in Pixie Hollow. Hook and his pirates never came to this part of Never Land's forest. And the fairies tried to avoid the pirates as much as they could. Just then, they heard a muffled boom from the direction of Pirate Cove. Several fairies jumped.

"Cannon fire," said Queen Clarion. "Captain Hook must be after Peter Pan again."

The others knew what she meant. On Never Land, there was an on-and-off battle between Hook and his pirates and Peter and the Lost Boys. On certain quiet nights, when the wind was just right, the fairies could hear Pan's and Hook's swords clashing in the distance.

"*Hmm,*" said Tink with a worried frown. She didn't like to think of Captain Hook firing cannonballs at Peter.

But Peter is too quick and too clever to get hit by a cannonball, Tink assured herself.

There was another muffled boom, followed by a whizzing sound.

"Everyone, duck!" said the queen.

The fairies all dashed for cover in the roots of the Home Tree. Something flew through the air high over their heads. It landed in the nearby forest with a tremendous thud.

"The fairy circle!" cried Dulcie. She hurried out from behind a root. "What if it landed there?"

"What about Mother Dove?" Rani said, almost in a whisper. "What if it hit her hawthorn tree?"

The fairies looked at each other in stricken silence. Mother Dove was the closest thing to pure goodness in all of Never Land. She was the source of all the fairies' magic. They had almost lost her once, when a hurricane hit Never Land. The thought of losing her again was too dreadful to bear.

In a tense voice, Queen Clarion told several fast-flying fairies to fly to the hawthorn and check on Mother Dove. They zipped off in a blur.

Moments later, the fast fliers were back.

"Mother Dove is fine," a fast-flying sparrow man reported. "Not one feather ruffled. And the fairy circle is undamaged."

The fairies let out a collective sigh of relief.

Just then, Spring, a messenger-talent fairy, came speeding up to Tink. "I've just been to the top of the Home Tree," she said grimly. "You'd better come with me."

Chapter 3

*W*hat now? Tink wondered.

She followed the messenger into the Home Tree. They passed through the main corridor, where paintings representing each different Never fairy talent hung on the walls. Tink saw that most of the paintings were crooked. Some had even fallen to the floor. She stopped and straightened the painting of a dented stewpot, which was the symbol for the pots-and-pans talent.

Up through the branches they went. Finally, they came to the corridor that led to Tink's room. Tink saw her friend Terence waiting for her. Terence had been in the group the queen had sent to check the damage to the tree. He looked upset.

"Tink," he said, "I hardly know how to tell you this. Your bedroom—"

Tink didn't even wait for him to finish his sentence. She zoomed down the corridor to the end of the branch where her room sat. What would she find? she wondered. Would it be a horrible mess? Would her loaf-pan bed be overturned, or even dented? It was not a pleasant thought.

When she reached the tip of the branch, she stopped cold.

Her room wasn't a mess. Her room wasn't there at all.

Tinker Bell hovered, staring. The walls, the ceiling, and everything in the room had disappeared. All that remained was the floor and the jagged edges of the broken walls.

She looked up past the hole where her ceiling should have been. The surrounding branches had a few broken twigs. But the other fairies' rooms were still there. The cannonball had hit Tink's room, and Tink's alone.

Tink felt faint. She sat down cross-legged on the floor.

How could my room just be...gone? she thought. *Where will I sleep? Where will I keep my clothes and other things? Where are my clothes and other things?*

More fairies began to arrive to see what had happened.

"Oh, Tink," said her friend Beck. "It's awful!"

"I can't believe it," said Prilla. "Your bed is gone. And it was such a great bed."

Tink stood up. She didn't want the other fairies to feel sorry for her. She took a deep breath. "We'll just rebuild it," she said. She sounded calmer than she felt. "And it will be an even better room than before."

"We'll all help you," said Terence. The others nodded in agreement.

Suddenly Tink felt angry. After all, no one would have to rebuild anything if it weren't for the cannonball. "And in the meantime," she said fiercely, "we're going to get that horrid cannonball out of our courtyard. What do you say, fairies?"

"Yes!" they all cried. "Let's do it!"

With Tink in the lead, the fairies went

back to the courtyard. The most obvious thing was to try pushing the cannonball, Tink decided. "If a lot of us get behind it and fly as hard as we can, maybe we can roll it out of the courtyard," she said.

"Let's move every little twig out of its path. That way it won't get stuck on anything," said Beck.

The cleaning-talent fairies grabbed their brooms and swept up all the splinters. Other fairies helped by moving the pieces of the squashed mushroom chairs.

"All right," said Tink. "Let's get into pushing formation."

Several fairies arranged themselves behind the ball.

"One, two, three...*shove!*" shouted Tink.

The fairies beat their wings madly. They heaved against the ball as hard as they could.

After a moment, they stopped. Several fairies leaned against the ball, panting.

"It didn't move an inch," said Angus.

"Let's give it another try," said Tink. "One, two, three...*shove!*"

The fairies used every ounce of strength they had. At last they stopped. Their wings were quivering with exhaustion.

"Nothing," said Angus.

Indeed, the ball had not moved, not a hair.

Tink sighed. "Well, I guess that's not going to work," she said. "But this is only the beginning."

Chapter 4

Because the kitchen was such a mess, dinner that night was simple—acorn-butter sandwiches with dandelion salad. The tired fairies ate quickly. The sun had already set. After a long, hard day of work, they were eager to go to bed.

As soon as she was done eating, Tink realized she had a problem. She had nowhere to sleep. She watched as the other fairies headed for their rooms. In all the excitement over the cannonball, they had forgotten that Tink didn't have her own room to go to.

The tearoom slowly emptied. Tink remained sitting at her table. She wasn't sure what to do. As the shadows lengthened, she felt more and more forlorn.

At last Rani noticed Tink sitting alone. She realized the problem at once.

"Tink," she said, "what will you do tonight?"

"I think maybe I'll just sleep outside," Tink replied. "I can use a maple leaf as a blanket."

"You can sleep in my room," Rani told her. "It's better than sleeping outside, anyway."

"Okay," Tink said. She felt relieved. "I would like that. I'm awfully tired."

Tink followed Rani up to her room.

She had visited Rani's room many times before. But until that evening, she hadn't noticed the details. She looked around at the blue-green walls and the seaweed curtains hanging in the windows. The floor was paved with smooth river stones. It seemed like a quiet, peaceful place. Tink was looking forward to a good night's sleep.

"Shall we play a game of seashell tiddly-winks?" Rani asked.

"Not tonight," said Tink. "I think I'm ready to go to bed. Where should I sleep?"

"I could pile lots of blankets on the floor," Rani suggested.

"Let me help you," said Tink.

Together they piled woven-fern blankets on the floor until they had made a soft bed.

"That should be very comfortable," Tink said when they were done. But she could not help noticing how humid Rani's room was. Even the blankets felt damp.

Tink settled herself on the pile. She was so tired, she was sure she'd fall asleep in a moment.

Rani covered her up with a sheet, which was also slightly damp. "Good night, dear friend," she said. Then she climbed into her own bed, which was made from driftwood. She pulled the seaweed quilt up to her chin.

Tink lay on her back, gazing at the blue-green ceiling. *It was nice of Rani to take me in*, she thought. Then she closed her eyes and gave in to her tiredness.

Seconds later, Tink opened her eyes. She could feel a lump beneath the pile of blankets. It was one of the river stones that paved the floor.

Tink tried turning on her side, but that was no better. She flopped over on her stomach, but that was worse still. She ended up on her back again.

Tink thought wistfully of her comfy loaf-pan bed. How she loved to fall asleep beneath the still life of the stockpot, whisk, and griddle. And now it was gone.

Moonlight filtered in through the seaweed curtains. Suddenly Tink gasped and jumped up. Two long arms seemed to reach out to her from the corner of the room.

Rani heard her and sat straight up. "What's the matter?" she cried.

"Th-there's something in the corner!" whispered Tink. She was almost too scared to breathe.

"Where? I don't see it!" whispered Rani. She followed the direction of Tink's pointing finger. But the room was too dark. They couldn't see clearly.

Quickly, Rani lit her scallop-shell lamp. Then she started to giggle. "That's just my clothes hanging on a clothes tree, Tink. It's made from a coral branch. Remember?"

Gradually, Tink's heart stopped racing. Her breath returned to normal. "Oh," she said. "So it is." Now she felt foolish. She wished more than ever that she could be in her own bed.

Rani turned out the light. They settled back down to sleep.

Drip. Drip. Drip-drip. Drip. Drip. Drip. Drip-drip. Drip.

It was a slow, steady rhythm. Tink had forgotten all about Rani's drip. She had a permanent leak in her room, whether it was raining or not. Beneath the leak sat a bucket made from a human-sized thimble. Inside the bucket, a Never minnow swam contentedly around and around.

Drip. Drip. Drip-drip. Drip.

By now, Tink had given up trying to sleep. She lay on her back and stared at the ceiling. Every now and then she shifted her wings under the damp sheet to find a better position.

A little after dawn, Rani awoke. She sat up in bed and stretched her arms toward the ceiling. "I just had the most wonderful night's sleep, and the most wonderful dream!" she said when she saw that Tink was awake.

Tink sighed. She was glad her friend had slept well, but she hadn't slept a wink.

Chapter 5

Breakfast was very good, as usual. Platters of Dulcie's wonderful pumpkin muffins and pots of blackberry tea sat on every table in the tearoom. But no breakfast would have been delicious enough to cheer up Tink that morning.

Tink was tired. And she wanted her room back.

She stared gloomily at the serving platter

in front of her. It reminded her of her platter–frying-pan–spoon chair.

"Rough night?" asked Angus. He was sitting next to Tink at the pots-and-pans-talent table.

"Just a little tired," said Tink with a sigh. She took a sip of tea. "But don't worry. I'm ready to get to work. I'll have that cannonball out of Pixie Hollow in no time." Even to her own ears, she did not sound very sure.

"Tinker Bell!" a cheerful voice exclaimed. Tink turned around. Gwinn, a tiny decoration-talent fairy, was beaming at her. "Are you ready to start putting your room back together?" Gwinn asked. "Cedar and I are heading up there now to get started." She gestured at Cedar, who was standing behind her. Cedar was the biggest, strongest-looking fairy Tinker Bell had ever seen. She was nearly six inches tall!

It was clear from the hammer and saw Cedar was carrying that she was a carpenter-talent. Cedar nodded shyly in greeting. Her great height made Gwinn look even tinier.

"Usually, we prepare rooms for fairies who have just arrived in Never Land," Gwinn continued. She spoke very, very fast. Tink had to concentrate to keep up. "Of course, we don't know them yet. So we just make our best guess about what that fairy might want. And then we hope she likes it. But you're already *here*! I've never helped a fairy decorate her own room before! You can tell me exactly what you want! It will be perfect! *Perfect!* Right, Cedar?"

Cedar nodded and stared bashfully at the ground.

Tink bit her lip. She wanted to start rebuilding her room. But she had promised to get rid of the cannonball.

Angus read her mind. "You can work on the cannonball later, Tink, after you and Gwinn decide what your new room should look like," he pointed out.

Tink thought about it for a moment. Angus was right. The cannonball could wait.

"All right," Tink said. She smiled. "Let's go!"

A short time later, Tink was watching Cedar hammer planks into the walls of her new room. Gwinn flew from one corner to the next, measuring the space with her eyes.

She kept up a steady stream of chatter. "You'll want silver paint," Gwinn told Tink. "Or maybe gold. Or something copper? *Ooh*, yes! Copper could be just lovely with the sunlight coming in—"

"Silver will be fine," said Tink, trying to keep up.

"And I suppose you'd like colander lampshades again," Gwinn went on. "Although a nice iris-petal lantern would give the room a softer look…"

"Colanders, please," Tink cut in. She was surprised to find she was having fun.

"And you'll need curtains, a bedspread, some kind of rug…" Gwinn zipped from corner to corner. She was making Tink dizzy.

Tink sat down in the middle of the bare floor to watch her.

Gwinn will make sure that the walls are the right color, Tink thought. *And she will get new colanders for the lamps.* But Gwinn couldn't make her another still-life painting. And Cedar couldn't make her another loaf-pan bed.

If I want my room back just the way it was, Tink thought, *I'm going to have to take matters into my own hands.*

"I'll be back in a little while," she told Gwinn and Cedar.

Cedar mumbled good-bye through a mouthful of nails. Gwinn absentmindedly waved some curtain fabric at her. Tink flew out through the open ceiling and over the woods of Pixie Hollow.

Soon, Tink arrived at Bess's studio. It was made from an old tangerine crate that the art-talent fairy had set up in a remote clearing in the woods, where she could paint in peace and quiet.

Tink found Bess hard at work. She was painting a portrait of an animal-talent fairy. The animal-talent fairy posed on a cushion, holding her favorite ladybug on her lap.

"Tink!" Bess said. She set down her brush and hugged her friend. "What a terrible thing to happen to your room. Is there anything I can do to help?"

"Actually, there is," said Tink. She explained that she needed another still life of a stockpot, whisk, and griddle to hang over her bed.

Bess looked a little embarrassed. "Oh, Tink," she said unhappily. "Of *course* I'll paint a new picture for you. But I won't be able to get to it for a while. I've already promised paintings to five other fairies."

The animal-talent fairy cleared her throat impatiently. The ladybug on her lap was getting restless. Bess gave Tink another hug, and then got back to work.

Tink flew off, trying not to feel discouraged. Her next stop was the kitchen. She hoped to find some pots and pans that were beyond repair. With luck, she could make another frying-pan chair exactly like her old one.

Dulcie met Tink at the kitchen door. She was carrying a tray of pretty little tea cakes. As Dulcie set the cakes on a windowsill to cool, Tink asked her if she had any pots, pans, spoons, whisks, or other kitchen items that she needed to get rid of.

"Well," replied Dulcie, "there was that salad fork with the bent tines. I was ready to give up on it. But Angus fixed it last week.

It's been perfectly pointy and prongy ever since."

The other pots-and-pans fairies are too good at their jobs, Tink thought. She sighed in frustration. She didn't want to make a chair out of objects that were still useful.

Tink could usually fix almost anything. But here was something that couldn't be fixed, at least not right away.

"*Grrr!*" cried Tink. She shot three inches into the air with sheer frustration. Her room was smashed, and even when it was fixed, it still wouldn't feel like her room. After all, *where* was she going to find another loaf-pan bed?

That cannonball will regret the day it fell into Pixie Hollow, Tink vowed. *And Captain Hook will regret it even more.*

Chapter 6

Tink zoomed into the courtyard. She flew right up to the cannonball and gave it a mighty kick.

Ow! Tink danced through the air, clutching her toes and grimacing in pain. A few fairies who had been flying by stared at Tink in astonishment.

"This cannonball is going to move!" she cried. "I am going to banish it from Pixie Hollow once and for all. But I'm going to need help from every fairy and sparrow man. Together, we can do it! Now, who's with me?"

But the other fairies didn't jump up as Tink hoped they would.

"I don't know. Maybe we could learn to live with the cannonball," said one of the decoration-talent fairies. "We could probably fix it up to make it look nice."

The other decoration-talent fairies brightened a bit. "We could!" one agreed. "We could decorate it with hollyhock garlands and daisy chains."

"But...but don't you want to get rid of it?" Tink asked, astonished.

"Well, of course we do, Tink," said Beck, who happened to be in the courtyard. "But we want to get back to doing what we usually do. We're all busy with our own talents."

Tink couldn't believe what she was hearing. Were the other fairies giving up already, before they'd even tried?

"We have fun in the courtyard, don't we?" she said. "It's part of our home. How will we feel looking at this cannonball every time we come out of the Home Tree? We'll never be able to have a meeting or a party here again. Even if it's decorated and painted, it will still take up too much room."

Several fairies murmured in agreement. But no one volunteered to help.

"I know we can do this," Tink replied. "We just have to figure out how." Just then, Terence flew up. He was holding a teacup in one hand. In his other hand was a sack of fairy dust. "Tink, you didn't get your fairy dust yet today, did you?" he said. As a dust-talent sparrow man, Terence handed out dust to all the fairies and sparrow men in Pixie Hollow. Everyone got one teacupful per day. The dust was what allowed the fairies to fly and do magic.

As Terence poured the magical dust over Tink, her eyes widened. "That's it! I know how we can move the cannonball!" she cried.

The fairies in the courtyard perked up. "How, Tink?" Terence asked.

"We move big things with balloon carriers, right?" Tink said. Balloon carriers were baskets attached to fairy-dust-filled balloons. The fairies used them to move things that were too heavy to carry. "That's what we'll do with the cannonball. We'll build a giant balloon and use lots of extra fairy dust to give it more lift. We can float the cannonball away."

"It's a good idea," said Terence. The other fairies nodded. Even Angus looked impressed.

"Send word to the other dust-talent fairies," Tink told Terence. "We'll need all the fairy dust they can spare. The rest of us will get the balloon carrier ready."

This was easier said than done. In order to attach the balloon to the cannonball, they would need heavy ropes. Tink found Florian and explained her plan.

"We'll use marsh grass," Florian said with certainty. "And we'll make it extra thick."

She got the weaving-talent fairies together, and they set out to collect long strands of tough marsh grasses, which they would weave into the strongest ropes they could make. Next, Tink went to the sewing-talent

fairies. She asked them to make a silk balloon, the biggest one Pixie Hollow had ever
seen. Some of the fairies grumbled. They
didn't want to leave the pretty petal dresses
and leaf-frock coats they were working on.
But Tink's spirit was catching. Soon, they
were collecting every spare scrap of spider
silk to make the giant balloon. It was afternoon by the time the weaving-talent fairies finished making the ropes. They were
nearly as thick as a fairy's waist and looked
very sturdy. The weavers secured the ropes
around the bottom of the cannonball. Then
it was time to attach the balloon. The sewing-talent fairies sewed the ends of each rope
to the edges of the balloon.

Tink oversaw all this work. She paced
back and forth, worrying. Would the balloon lift off? Would the cannonball stay

attached? What if this idea didn't work, either?

At last, the whole contraption was ready to go. It was time for the dust-talent fairies and sparrow men to do their work.

By now a crowd had gathered. Everyone watched, hardly daring to breathe, as Terence and a dust-talent sparrow man named Jerome began to fill the balloon with fairy dust. Instead of the teacups they usually used to hand out the dust, they scooped up great mounds of it with shovels they had borrowed from the garden-talent fairies.

The balloon started to rise—up, up, up. The fairies watched in wonder. Soon the balloon was completely inflated. It strained against the ropes.

The ropes pulled taut, but the cannonball stayed stubbornly on the ground.

"More fairy dust!" cried Tink.

Terence and Jerome flew up to the top of the balloon and sprinkled more shovelfuls of dust onto it. They sprinkled some dust onto the cannonball for good measure. The balloon strained harder and harder. All the fairies and sparrow men strained with it. The fairies glowed brightly as they willed the balloon to rise.

And finally, it did! The grass ropes pulled tauter, and the cannonball could resist no longer. It lifted off the ground.

"It's going!" shouted Tink.

First it rose just a hair off the ground, no more than the thickness of a fairy's wing. Then it reached the height of two hairs. Then it was almost as high up as a fairy's knee, and then higher than a fairy's head. It was working! It was really working!

If the fairies and sparrow men had not been so caught up in the progress of the cannonball, they might have noticed that a strong breeze had sprung up. But they did not notice, until—

Pow! Hissssssss. "What was that?" Tink cried in alarm. What it was, they soon discovered, was a horse chestnut. The spiky green globe had fallen from a nearby horse chestnut tree. And the wind had been blowing in just the right direction to push it into the balloon. The horse chestnut's spikes had pierced the delicate spider silk.

The hissing lasted only a second. The cannonball landed back in the courtyard with a great thud. Inside the tree, delicate cups and saucers could be heard shattering in the tearoom.

The fairies groaned.

"Well, that's the end of that," Angus said.

But that wasn't the end. For the cannon-ball had gotten just the start it needed. It began to roll.

Chapter 7

he ball!" Rani cried. "L-look out!"
Several fairies leaped out of the
way in the nick of time. There was a very
slight slope away from the Home Tree, but
that was enough. The cannonball rolled
down it.

"Hooray!" a decoration-talent fairy yelled.
"Good-bye, ball!"

"Good riddance!" added a butterfly
herder.

But Tink followed the ball's progress, frowning.

"It's great that we got it going, but—" she began.

"Now we don't know *where* it's going," Rani finished for her.

"Exactly," said Tink.

The ball began to pick up speed. The fairies' cheers died out.

"It was so hard to start," Terence said worriedly. "But now it's going to be impossible to stop!"

"Maybe it will just roll into a tree or something," said Beck.

"If we're lucky," said Angus.

"I think we'd better follow it!" cried Tink. And the fairies leaped into the air to chase after the ball.

The cannonball was rolling fast now. It

bounced across a tree root and rolled over a hillock of grass. It was headed for Havendish Stream.

"It's going to hit the mill!" cried Jerome.

The mill was one of the most important places in Pixie Hollow. The tree-picking-talent fairies ground grains and nuts into baking flour there. And the dust-talent fairies used the mill to grind Mother Dove's feathers into fairy dust. It was also where the fairy dust was stored—all of it.

At once, the same picture flashed through every fairy's and sparrow man's mind: the mill smashed, the fairy dust inside blowing away with the wind. They would be unable to fly, unable to do magic. How would they even build another mill if they did not have the power of fairy dust?

A startled rabbit poked his head out of his burrow. But when he saw the cannonball rolling toward him, he quickly dove back inside.

The cannonball rolled over a large toadstool, flattening it. The fairies flew helplessly behind. They could hardly bring themselves to watch.

But just before it reached the mill, the cannonball hit a good-sized rock. It jumped into the air and changed course. Instead of crashing into the mill, the ball splashed into the stream just above it. And there it stopped, wedged against the bank.

The fairies breathed sighs of relief all around. They laughed and hugged each other with joy. The mill was saved!

But Tink was not laughing. She did

not take her eyes from the ball. As she watched, the water of Havendish Stream began to back up around it.

"Oh no!" she cried. "The stream is blocked!"

Everyone stared in disbelief. Tink was right. The ball had landed in the narrow branch of the stream that fed the mill. The water slowed to a trickle. If the stream stopped running, the mill wheel would stop turning.

Indeed, moments later they all heard the mill grind to a stop.

Rani started to cry, and it was not from happiness.

Why didn't I think of this? Tink asked herself angrily. *Why didn't it occur to me that once the ball started rolling, it was anybody's guess where it would end up?*

She sank down to the ground. She felt completely defeated. She had taken on a challenge that was too big. And she had failed. What was going to happen to Pixie Hollow now?

"Well, Tink," someone said. Tink looked up. Queen Clarion was standing next to her. "I guess it's time for you to come up with another idea," the queen said seriously.

This took Tink by surprise. She had thought the story was over. The ball was stuck in the stream. There was certainly no way to move it now.

But Rani was nodding and smiling through her tears. "We know you can figure this out, Tink," she said. "Look how many great ideas you've had. There has to be one more thing."

Tink was astounded. Not only did the

others have hope that the problem could be solved, they thought she could solve it.

Rani is right, she thought. *There has to be one more thing.* Tink knew she had a responsibility to figure out what that one thing was. The other fairies were counting on her.

"Yes, Tink," said Florian. "It's time for your next idea. Do you want us to leave you alone?"

"Or would you like some nice soup while you think?" said one of the cooking-talent fairies, who specialized in cucumber soup.

"No soup," Tink said, squaring her shoulders. "I'm just going to think."

Chapter 8

Tink flitted around the whole terrible scene, trying to focus. It was hard looking at the mess the cannonball had made. Water was starting to flood the banks of the stream, turning them into muddy pools. Toadstools and wildflowers had been squashed and flattened when the ball rolled over them. The cannonball had also plowed through a pile of acorns that the tree-picking-talent fairies had set aside to be ground in the mill. Now little chips of acorn littered the landscape.

Tink stared at them. They reminded her of something.

Little chips of acorn, she thought. *Little chips . . .*

"I've got it!" she hollered. "I've got the solution! I was thinking about it the wrong way the whole time! The cannonball is a huge thing, right?" said Tink. "It was much too heavy for us to move. And we certainly couldn't control it once it started moving. But even if we can't move a huge thing, we can move lots of *little* things."

Queen Clarion nodded her head in understanding. "Of course!" she said.

"Of course *what*?" said a few fairies who hadn't caught on.

"We're going to break the cannonball

into lots of tiny pieces and move them out of Pixie Hollow," Tink declared. "Spring!" She turned to the messenger-talent fairy. "Ask the other pots-and-pans fairies to bring all the hammers and chisels they have in their workshops. And the carpenter-talent fairies—they have hammers and chisels, too!"

"I have a couple of chisels," said an art-talent fairy. "For making sculptures."

"Great!" said Tink. "Let's round up all the tools we have. We're going to break this cannonball up!"

A short time later, an array of tools was laid out on the grass next to the cannonball. The sand-sorting-talent fairies had piled sandbags around the ball to hold back the stream. That way, the fairies wouldn't get wet as they worked.

Tink grabbed a hammer and chisel and flew to the top of the cannonball. As the best pots-and-pans fairy in Pixie Hollow, Tink knew a lot about metal. For example, she knew that every piece of metal had a weak point.

She put her ear close to the cannonball. Then she began to tap it with her hammer, inching across the surface.

Bing, bing, bing, bing, bing, bing, bing, bing, bing, bing, bong, bing...

Tink stopped. She went back and tapped the spot again.

Bong!

Tink had found the cannonball's weak spot. Holding the tip of her chisel against the ball, Tink whacked it with the hammer as hard as she could. A crack appeared.

Tink whacked it again. The crack grew.

"Everybody take a hammer and chisel!" Tink told the other fairies. "Even if your talent is completely unrelated to breaking up cannonballs, give it a try. You might like it."

The fairies got to work. As they wedged their chisels into the iron, more cracks appeared. The air started to ring with the sound of metal banging into metal. It was a sound Tink loved with all her heart.

"I like this!" said one of the cooking-talent fairies, whose specialty was making ice sculptures. "It's just like chipping ice. But you don't have to be careful!"

Gradually, the cracks in the cannonball grew. Pieces began to break off. The fairies laid them on the bank of Havendish Stream.

Soon they had broken the whole cannonball apart. A mound of iron bits sat by the stream.

"What are we going to do with all this?" said Twire, a scrap-metal-recovery-talent fairy. "It's more iron than we could use in an entire year in Pixie Hollow."

Tink nodded. But she wasn't really focused on what Twire was saying. She was getting another idea.

Quietly, she waved Terence over. "I want to ask your opinion about something," she said. "About fairy-dust magic." She whispered her idea into Terence's ear.

Terence scratched his head thoughtfully.

"I think it can be done," he said finally. "It will take a great deal of fairy dust. And the magic won't be easy. We'll have to concentrate. But I think it could work."

"That's what I hoped," said Tink.

She flew back to where the other fairies were still working. They were almost finished breaking apart the cannonball.

Tink stood on one of the bigger pieces of iron to make her announcement.

"Fairies," she said, "we're going to get this cannonball out of Pixie Hollow once and for all."

The fairies cheered.

"But what are we going to do with it?" asked Rani.

Tink smiled and said with a wink, "We're going to give it back to Captain Hook, of course."

Chapter 9

Shouting with glee, the fairies gathered up the pieces of cannonball. There were many more pieces than there were fairies. So each fairy took as many as she could fly with. Gwinn took one big piece. Cedar took six small ones. Tink herself carried three pieces, and it took all her strength to lift off.

Meanwhile, Jerome and Terence were inside the mill filling sacks full of fairy dust, as much as they could carry. When everything was ready, the fairies lifted into the air. It was quite a sight, for those who could see it: a great cloud of fairies flying over the lush landscape of Never Land, headed for Pirate Cove. Of course, the pirates themselves could not see the fairies, who were invisible to them. If Captain Hook had looked up just then, he would have seen hundreds of chips of iron miraculously bobbing through the air.

But Captain Hook was not looking up. As the fairies approached the cove, they could see the vile-tempered pirate rowing a small boat through the water near the shore. He was muttering to himself.

"I'll teach that ridiculous boy a lesson," he growled. "Throw my best cutlass into the sea, will he? Thinks he can get the best of me, does he? Well, we'll see about that, Master Peter Pan. Let's see how you like a cannonball for your dinner tonight."

As Hook rowed, he looked down through the shallow water.

The fairies were right above Hook's little rowboat. They hovered there, still in a cloud. "Okay!" Tink cried. "Start bringing the pieces together!"

The fairies flew nearer to each other. They began to fit the pieces of cannonball together.

"Now the fairy dust!" Tink commanded.

Terence and the other dust-talent fairies and sparrow men began to throw handfuls of fairy dust over the ball. Magically, the iron chips snapped into place like pieces of a jigsaw puzzle. The fairies concentrated, using all the magic they could muster.

In moments, the cannonball was complete. It was just as it had been when it crashed into Pixie Hollow.

And, of course, once it was whole, it was too heavy for the fairies to hold any longer. It fell from their grasp and plummeted toward Captain Hook's rowboat.

Hook looked up just in time to see a cannonball fall from thin air.

"What—" was all he had time to say before the ball crashed into the floor of his rowboat. It broke through the wood and fell to the bottom of the sea.

At once, the boat filled with water. Hook had no choice but to abandon ship. He swam to shore as the rowboat slowly sank. The sun was setting as the fairies flew back to Pixie Hollow, glad to finally be rid of the cannonball.

✦   ✦   ✦

The next day, Pixie Hollow had just about returned to normal. Havendish Stream flowed between its banks, which looked none the worse for wear. The mill was turning once again. And fairies from several different talents had pitched in to help repair the courtyard. The cooking-talent fairies had spent the day making acorn soup, muffins, cookies, and bread with the acorns that had been smashed by the cannonball. Everyone was good and sick of acorns. But all the broken ones had been just about used up, and nothing had gone to waste. After her sleepless night in Rani's room, Tink had decided to sleep outside until her room was rebuilt. She'd found a nook between two branches where she would be sheltered from the wind and safe from owls. She had actually been quite happy out there, looking at the stars through the leaves of the Home Tree. And in the morning, what had she found by the roots of a nearby tree but her loaf-pan bed! It had one big dent in it. *Challenging to fix,* Tink thought. *But not too challenging.*

✦   ✦   ✦

Later that day, Gwinn and Cedar helped Tink carry the bed up to her new room. They had worked all night to get it ready for her.

When Gwinn opened the door, Tink was speechless with delight. Her new room had colander lamps just like the old ones. The walls were painted with silver paint to make them look as if they were made of tin. And best of all, Bess had managed to finish a new painting for Tink after all. It was another still life of a stockpot, whisk, and griddle—and it was twice the size of the old one.

"It's beautiful," she managed to say at last.

Gwinn and Cedar helped Tink put her bed back into place. Then Gwinn took another look around the room. "You know," she said thoughtfully, "we could decorate with tiny cannonballs, Tink. So you'd always remember your greatest challenge."

"It's an interesting thought," said Tink. "But I'm all through with cannonballs."

Just then, Dulcie came hurrying up to Tink's room. She poked her head in the open door and waved a metal sheet.

"Tink," she said, "do you think you

could fix this baking sheet for me? I have one last batch of acorn cookies to put in the oven. It just has a little hole. I know it's hardly worth your attention. Not much of a challenge."

"Believe me," said Tink, "that is just fine with me."

And taking the sheet from Dulcie's hands, she headed for her workshop, whistling.

If you enjoyed *Tinker Bell's* FAIRYTASTIC READING ADVENTURE, don't miss…

Available now.